# EASTER CRACK-UPS

## Knock-Knock Jokes
### Funny-Side Up

By Katy Hall and Lisa Eisenberg
Pictures by Steve Björkman

HARPER FESTIVAL
An Imprint of HarperCollinsPublishers

Knock, knock!
  Who's there?
Heidi.
  Heidi who?
Heidi eggs under the bushes!

Knock, knock!
  Who's there?
Lettuce.
  Lettuce who?
Lettuce hide some
more eggs over here!

Knock, knock!
Who's there?
Stan.
Stan who?

Stan back and I'll toss you an egg!

Knock, knock!
Who's there?
Quack.
Quack who?
Quack the egg and you're
out of the game.

Knock, knock!
Who's there?
Eggs.
Eggs who?
Eggs-actly where is the finish line?

Knock, knock!
  Who's there?
Ivan.
  Ivan who?
Ivan to give you the prize!

Knock, knock!
  Who's there?

Andrew.
  Andrew who?
Andrew a bunny on her egg.

Knock, knock!
  Who's there?
Ears.
    Ears who?
Ears a good spot
to hide some eggs!

Knock, knock!
  Who's there?
Adam.
    Adam who?
Adam up and see who has the most eggs!

Knock, knock!
  Who's there?
Sarah.
  Sarah who?
Sarah way to stick this
bow to my bonnet?

Knock, knock!
  Who's there?
Tuba.
  Tuba who?
Tuba glue's
what you need.

Knock, knock!
Who's there?
Sherwood.
Sherwood who?

Sherwood like to be in the Easter parade.

Knock, knock!
Who's there?
Ketchup.
Ketchup who?

Ketchup to the person
in front of you!

Knock, knock!
 Who's there?
Abby.
 Abby who?